The Nutcracker

Michael Hague

chronicle books · san francisco

For Brittany and Jim
from Michael and Kathleen

This edition published in 2005 by Chronicle Books LLC.

Text © 2003 by Chronicle Books LLC.
Illustrations © 2003 by Michael Hague.
All rights reserved.

Story written by Sarah L. Thomson.
Book design by Nicole de las Heras and Ellen Friedman.
The illustrations in this book were rendered in pen and ink, watercolor, and colored pencils.
Manufactured in China.
ISBN 0-8118-5027-7

The Library of Congress has cataloged the previous edition as follows:
Hague, Michael.
The nutcracker / Michael Hague [illustrator; text, Sarah L. Thomson].
p. cm.
Summary: In this adaptation of the original 1816 German story, with elements from the ballet, Godfather
Drosselmeier gives young Marie a nutcracker for Christmas, and she finds herself in a magical realm where
she saves a boy from an evil curse.
ISBN 1-58717-254-2 (Paperback)—ISBN 1-58717-255-0 (Library binding)
[1. Nutcrackers (Implements)—Fiction. 2. Toys—Fiction. 3. Christmas—Fiction. 4. Fairy tales.] I.
Thomson, Sarah L. II. Hoffmann, E. T. A. (Ernst Theodor Amadeus), 1776-1822. Nussknacker und
Mausekonig. III. Nutcracker (Choreographic work) IV. Title.

PZ8.H126Nu 2003
[Fic]—dc21
2003042749

Distributed in Canada by Raincoast Books
9050 Shaughnessy Street, Vancouver, British Columbia V6P 6E5

10 9 8 7 6 5 4 3 2 1

Chronicle Books LLC
85 Second Street, San Francisco, California 94105

www.chroniclekids.com

On Christmas Eve, Marie and her

little brother Fritz sat together in a small back room while
their parents were busy in the front parlor. In that room, Marie
and Fritz knew, there was a Christmas tree taller than their
father, a table spread with a feast, and presents wrapped in
crisp paper and tied with bright red bows. But Marie and Fritz
were not allowed inside until everything was ready.

It was a little cold in the back parlor, for the fire had burned down, and a little dark, for the servants were too busy to come and light the candles. Marie and Fritz had started to think that the Christmas party would *never* be ready when they heard footsteps in the hall.

"Mama! Is it time? May we go inside?" Marie cried, running to the door. But it was not her mother. It was Godfather Drosselmeier.

Godfather Drosselmeier swept into the room, wearing his long black coat that wrapped around him like a bat's wings. He kissed Marie and shook hands with Fritz.

"Have you brought us presents, Godfather Drosselmeier?" Fritz demanded. For Godfather Drosselmeier was a watchmaker and always made them wonderful gifts: dolls that danced, horses that ran, castles with drawbridges that went up and down.

"Patience!" said Godfather Drosselmeier. "It's not time for presents yet. I've come to wait with you, and while we wait, I'll tell you a story."

And this is the tale Godfather Drosselmeier told:

Once upon a time, there lived a king and queen who had the most beautiful baby daughter in the world. Her name was Princess Pirlipat.

This king and queen were happy and wise and kind rulers of their land. But they had one problem: their castle had far too many rats. So they called in the royal watchmaker, whose name happened to be Drosselmeier. The watchmaker built such clever traps that none but two rats escaped: the Rat Queen and her seven-headed son, the King of the Rats. The Rat Queen was so furious that she cast a spell on poor Princess Pirlipat. In an instant, the baby changed: her head grew big and heavy, her eyes became wide and staring, and her mouth stretched from ear to ear.

Only Watchmaker Drosselmeier knew how to break the spell. For fifteen years he searched high and low for the fabulous Krackatuck nut, until he found it at last. "This nut," he said to the king, "must be cracked between the teeth of a young man who has never shaved, and that young man must take seven steps backward without stumbling. Then all will be well."

Fortunately, Watchmaker Drosselmeier had a young nephew who had never shaved and whose teeth were exceptionally hard. This young man, Frederick, cracked the nut between his teeth and handed the sweet kernel to the hideous Princess Pirlipat. She ate it and was in an instant her true self, with clear blue eyes, long golden braids, and a beaming smile.

Then, just as his uncle had told him, Frederick took six steps backward without stumbling. But as he took the seventh step, his foot came down on a black rat. It was the Queen Rat herself, and she squealed in triumph as Frederick stumbled and fell.

Frederick was not hurt in the least, but when he got up again, he looked just as Princess Pirlipat had, with a giant head, wide staring eyes, and a gaping mouth. The Rat Queen's spell now rested on Frederick.

"Take that hideous thing away!" cried Princess Pirlipat. "I cannot bear to look at him!"

So, despite all they had done for the royal family, Watchmaker Drosselmeier and his nephew left the court in disgrace. In time the Rat Queen died, but even then her spell was not lifted. Drosselmeier knew that her son, the Rat King, must also die if the spell were to be broken. And even that might not be enough.

Poor Frederick," said Marie. "Will he ever be free of the spell?"

"No one knows," said her godfather mysteriously, peering at Marie from under his bushy white eyebrows.

Just then, Marie's mother called from the front room. "Children! Come now! It's time!"

The Christmas tree rose nearly to the ceiling, and dozens of glowing candles nestled in its dark green branches. On a table there was a feast just for the children: gingerbread, walnuts and almonds, tiny flowers made of marzipan, peppermint sticks, and chocolate drops. And piled all around the tree were the presents.

There was a new dress for Marie, red velvet with a white lace collar. There was a hobbyhorse for Fritz, with bright button eyes and a handsome black mane. There were books for them both, with pictures of kings and castles and dragons.

At last, when they had opened all their other presents, Godfather Drosselmeier swept out two more boxes from behind his back. "One for each," he said with an elegant bow, handing the boxes to Marie and Fritz.

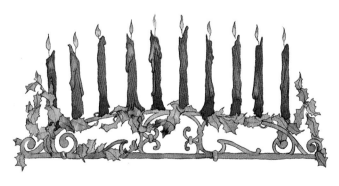

Fritz's box was full of toy soldiers. Some had horses to ride, some had cannons to pull, and they all had muskets and swords. Marie's present was a soldier of a different sort: a funny wooden doll with a head too big for his shoulders, wide eyes, and a huge mouth. He wore a bright red coat and had a sword by his side. Godfather Drosselmeier showed Marie how her doll could crack nuts between his strong white teeth.

"A nutcracker!" said Fritz. "He's nothing but an ugly old nutcracker!"

Nutcracker *was* ugly, Marie had to admit it. But he had such a bright smile and such a friendly look in his eyes that she loved him right away.

"Let me try him!" said Fritz. He snatched Nutcracker from Marie's arms.

"No!" said Marie. "You'll break him!"

But Marie was too late. Fritz had already shoved a giant walnut into Nutcracker's mouth and tried to crack it. The nut held firm, but Nutcracker's jaw cracked instead and two of his teeth fell out.

"Poor Nutcracker!" cried Marie. And when Fritz, who was truly sorry, handed the doll back to her, she held him in her arms and burst into tears. With two of his teeth missing, Nutcracker was uglier than ever.

"Don't cry, Marie," whispered Godfather Drosselmeier. "Tomorrow I'll come and mend Nutcracker. He'll be as good as new."

Then Marie's parents declared that is was bedtime. All the new toys were put away carefully in a cupboard. But as Marie lay in bed, she couldn't stop thinking of poor Nutcracker, all alone. At last she crept downstairs and made her way to the front parlor.

The candles on the Christmas tree were out and the room was dark and cold. Marie hurried to the toy cupboard and took out Nutcracker. Carefully she bandaged up his cracked jaw with a white ribbon from her hair. As Marie placed Nutcracker back in the cupboard, she heard the clock over the mantel strike midnight. Looking up, she was startled to see Godfather Drosselmeier perched on the clock with his black coat wrapped tightly around him!

Before Marie had a chance to call out to her godfather, a rat raced across the floor, scratching and scurrying, skittering and scrambling. Another leaped out from a corner, and a third dropped down from the curtains. Then there were more rats than Marie could count. Their claws went *scritch, scratch* on the wooden floor, and a hundred tiny voices squeaked and hissed, "The King! The King is coming!"

Suddenly the walls around Marie seemed to spring upward and the furniture grew larger. Soon the Christmas tree towered over her as if she were the size of a doll. But Marie hardly noticed, for her attention was seized by something creeping out from the shadows underneath the Christmas tree.

It was the largest rat Marie had ever seen. It stood on its hind legs and in one paw it held a small, sharp sword. And strangest of all, it had seven heads, and each of its seven heads wore a tiny golden crown. Each of its seven mouths showed sharp white teeth, and all fourteen of its eyes gleamed red in the darkness as it came closer and closer to Marie.

Just as Marie was about to scream, the door of the toy cupboard burst open. A small, brave figure leaped to the ground. "Never fear!" Nutcracker cried. "I'll do battle in your honor, sweet lady. All toys, follow me!"

Nutcracker tied Marie's white ribbon over his shoulder. Leaping off the shelves, all of Fritz's toy soldiers lined up behind him. The toy horses jumped down to serve as cavalry, and several dolls scrambled up on the table to fling down handfuls of walnuts and almonds to use as ammunition.

First the rats advanced. Nutcracker's troops marched out to meet them. The toy cannons banged and boomed, and the rats scattered as hard-shelled nuts rained down upon them. But they quickly gathered their ranks together and leaped on the toy soldiers, biting at their wooden limbs while the soldiers fought back with their swords. And the Nutcracker himself advanced on the Rat King.

Marie knelt by the toy cupboard with her hands over her mouth. All seven heads of the Rat King hissed with rage as he swung his sword at Nutcracker. Nutcracker fought back bravely, but his wooden limbs were stiff and slow. At last the Rat King knocked Nutcracker to the ground and raised his sword high.

"No!" sobbed Marie. Taking off her slipper, she hurled it straight at the Rat King, sending him staggering.

Nutcracker leaped up, seized his
sword, and, with one stroke, killed
the terrible Rat King.

All the other rats squealed with terror and fled, and Nutcracker's brave army raised a cheer. Nutcracker himself came to kneel at Marie's feet.

"Thank you, sweet lady, for saving my life," he said solemnly. "Please do me the honor of coming with me to my home, the Land of Toys, where there will be much rejoicing over the death of the Rat King."

"But how shall we get there?" asked Marie.

"This way, my lady," said the Nutcracker, and he swept aside the brocade curtains that hung at one of the windows.

Behind them rose a staircase to the windowsill that did
not lead outside into the cold winter's night, but rather to a
beautiful sunlit meadow.

A shining white path wound through tall green grass and
flowers made of spun sugar. Marie and Nutcracker crossed a
gingerbread bridge over a brook of lemonade and came at last
in sight of Nutcracker's city. All around the city were walls

made of marzipan, white as marble. As Marie and Nutcracker
passed through the gates, trumpeters blew their horns and
Nutcracker cried out, "The wicked Rat King is dead!"

All around Marie people clapped and cheered, and a crowd
danced and sang as they followed Marie and Nutcracker to the
castle. Everyone was dressed just like the dolls Marie had at
home; there were ballerinas and soldiers, clowns and brides,
and ladies in beautiful gowns.

At the palace, Nutcracker introduced Marie to all his court. "She saved my life!" he said. The whole court cheered to thank Marie, and a splendid feast was prepared for her. Marie nibbled on creamy fudge and sweet peppermint sticks while musicians played and dancers entertained her.

First a black-haired dancer spread her ruffled skirt in a deep curtsy as she placed a cup of steaming hot chocolate before Marie. Then two new dancers spun and leaped in a mist of soft veils, and Marie smelled coffee as they whirled past. The pair who came next wore robes that shone like gold, and they knelt to pour a cup of sweet tea for Nutcracker.

Then a Russian folk dance made Marie's hands clap and her feet twitch. She could hardly tell if the dancers who followed were flowers or fairies, but they flew like bright petals tossed on a spring wind.

Finally it was time for the last dance of all. "The Sugar Plum Fairy," Nutcracker whispered to Marie. The fairy and her prince moved like snowflakes drifting gently through the air.

When the feast was over, Nutcracker bowed to Marie and said, "Sweet lady, will you honor me with a waltz?"

While they danced, the music seemed to lift Marie's feet off the floor. She closed her eyes happily and the melody drifted away, becoming softer and sweeter as it faded in the distance. And when she opened her eyes again, she was in her own bed, with her mother bending over her.

Silly child!" said Marie's mother. "We found you sleeping beside the toy cupboard. You might have caught a terrible cold lying on the floor."

And when Marie told her all that had happened, her mother only smiled and said, "That was a beautiful dream, Marie, but now it's time to wake up. Godfather Drosselmeier is coming to visit."

Marie was sure that Godfather Drosselmeier would believe her, so she dressed quickly and ran downstairs. And there in the toy cupboard was Nutcracker!

"I thought you'd gone home to the Land of Toys," Marie said softly to him. "How can you still be here?"

But Nutcracker only stood stiff as wood and didn't answer a word.

Puzzled, Marie took Nutcracker in her arms and curled up in a big armchair to wait for Godfather Drosselmeier. Had it only been a dream?

As she sat waiting, she studied Nutcracker's friendly, ugly face, and she remembered Godfather Drosselmeier's story from the night before. Poor Frederick must have looked very much like Nutcracker, with his staring eyes and his big mouth. "If *you* were under a spell," she whispered to Nutcracker, "I'd never behave like that ungrateful Princess Pirlipat. I'd love you no matter how you looked!"

In that instant, a loud bang sounded in Marie's ears, and the room seemed to give such a jolt that she fell off her chair. When she got to her feet again, Nutcracker was nowhere to be found!

She had no time to look for him, for just then her mother came into the room. "Marie, here is Godfather Drosselmeier and his nephew, Frederick," she said. "Use your best manners and say hello."

With Godfather Drosselmeier was a young man, wearing a bright red coat with a sword at his side. Marie saw the same friendly look in his eyes as there had been in Nutcracker's. Then she knew that Godfather Drosselmeier's story had been true and that the spell was broken at last.

Many years later Marie and Frederick were married. Some say that Frederick became a watchmaker like his uncle. But others think that he and Marie still rule the Land of Toys to this day. On Christmas Eve, they say, you can make your way there, if you have eyes to see the way and courage for the journey.

A Note about the Story

Most people think of *The Nutcracker* as a Christmas ballet—but that's not how it began. The German author E. T. A. Hoffmann wrote *The Nutcracker and the Mouse King* in 1816. In this long story, a girl named Marie receives a nutcracker as a Christmas present from her mysterious godfather, Herr Drosselmeier. Marie doesn't know that the nutcracker is actually Drosselmeier's nephew. To free the boy from the spell that has trapped him in the shape of a toy, the seven-headed Mouse King must be killed and someone must love Nutcracker faithfully despite his ugly face.

In 1844, Alexandre Dumas (the author of *The Three Musketeers*) wrote a French version of Hoffmann's story called *The Nutcracker of Nuremburg*. And in 1891 the director and the choreographer of the Imperial Theater in St. Petersburg, Russia, used Dumas's text as a basis for a ballet, *The Nutcracker*. Pytor Ilich Tchaikovsky composed the music that has since become a classic.

In ballet form, the story became much simpler. The heroine (now called Clara) remained, along with the brave Nutcracker. The Mouse King became the Rat King. But the story-within-a-story that explained the true identity of the Nutcracker was lost. And the ballet introduced some new elements never present in Hoffmann's text—particularly the dances performed to entertain Clara by subjects in Nutcracker's kingdom and the Sugar Plum Fairy.

This version of *The Nutcracker* retains the shape and structure of the original Hoffmann story, but incorporates the elements of the ballet that readers will know and love.